P9-DHP-202

DATE DUE

MAR 13 1979	APR 21 1980	MAR 25 '94
MAR 20 1979	SEP 9	MAY 5 '94
MAR 23 1979	SEP 9 1980	DEC 16 '94
OCT 24 1980	APR 12 1979	SEP 19 1980	SEP 1 2 1995
DEC 12 1980	APR 13 1979	SEP 25 1980	NOV 2 6 1995
JAN 18 1980	SEP 20 1979	OCT 2 1980	OCT 8 '99
MAR 13 1981	OCT 30 1979	NOV 13 1980	
NOV 20 1981	JAN 29 1980	DEC 8 1980	

Fic
Cor

Corbett, Scott

The hockey trick

DATE	ISSUED TO

WASHINGTON TOWNSHIP
ELEMENTARY SCHOOL LIBRARY

THE HOCKEY TRICK

An Atlantic Monthly Press Book

LITTLE, BROWN AND COMPANY • Boston • Toronto

THE HOCKEY TRICK

by
Scott Corbett

illustrated by
Paul Galdone

WASHINGTON TOWNSHIP
ELEMENTARY SCHOOL LIBRARY

COPYRIGHT © 1974 BY SCOTT CORBETT

ALL RIGHTS RESERVED. NO PART OF THIS BOOK MAY BE REPRODUCED IN ANY FORM OR BY ANY ELECTRONIC OR MECHANICAL MEANS INCLUDING INFORMATION STORAGE AND RETRIEVAL SYSTEMS WITHOUT PERMISSION IN WRITING FROM THE PUBLISHER, EXCEPT BY A REVIEWER WHO MAY QUOTE BRIEF PASSAGES IN A REVIEW.

SECOND PRINTING

T 10/74

LIBRARY OF CONGRESS CATALOGING IN PUBLICATION DATA
Corbett, Scott.
  The hockey trick.

  "An Atlantic Monthly Press book."
  [1. Hockey—Fiction] I. Galdone, Paul, illus.
II. Title.
PZ7.C79938Hm   [Fic]   74-5022
ISBN 0-316-15716-3

ATLANTIC–LITTLE, BROWN BOOKS
ARE PUBLISHED BY
LITTLE, BROWN AND COMPANY
IN ASSOCIATION WITH
THE ATLANTIC MONTHLY PRESS

Published simultaneously in Canada
by Little, Brown & Company (Canada) Limited

PRINTED IN THE UNITED STATES OF AMERICA

To Ed "Army" Armstrong, master of puckish humor

1

KERBY MAXWELL pulled open the clubhouse door to let sunshine slant in.

"Might as well air it out while we can," he told Fenton.

The clubhouse in the center of the vacant lot had been built by the three boys who lived nearest to it. Fenton Claypool lived on one side of the lot, Bumps Burton on the other, and Kerby lived behind it.

Kerby's dog Waldo trotted inside the small shanty, gave the premises several good sniffs, and came out with nothing alarming to report. Like the rest of them, he was very fond of their meeting place.

It was one of those balmy days, late in February, that provides a sneak preview of spring. There was still a patch of snow on the roof, and another behind the clubhouse on the north side, but otherwise, no sign of winter remained.

"Won't be long now till the Panthers take the field," said Fenton, speaking of their baseball team.

"Play ball!" yelled Kerby, and swung an imaginary bat. "I can hardly wait!"

"Well, at least we won't have to start the season a man short. I thought we were going to be in real trouble when Pat Flanagan moved away. It's lucky Bumps grabbed that new kid for our team."

"Red Blake is still jumping up and down about that," said Kerby, grinning as he mentioned the redheaded, fiery-tempered captain of a rival team. "He's still talking about how we raided their neighborhood."

"I know. It's just too bad Louie's family didn't buy Pat's house, instead of one across the street. Then there wouldn't have been any argument."

The situation was complicated.

The street in question, Pickett Avenue, was the natural dividing line between the Panthers' neighborhood and the Wildcats'.

Every boy on the Wildcat team lived on the other side of Pickett Avenue. And until Bumps grabbed the new kid to replace Pat, every Panther had lived on *their* side of the avenue.

"But anyway, we've got Louie, and Red will just have to lump it," said Fenton.

He was a tall, thin boy who stood very straight and looked very solemn and was so fair and square about things he was sometimes hard to live with — but where baseball was concerned he could be as one-sided as the next fellow.

"Red's still got a full team," he went on, "he didn't need Louie Landowski, and we did."

"Besides, who says Louie is such a bargain?" sighed Kerby. "From what I've seen of him so far, he may give Butterfingers Blatweiler a run for Least Valuable Player. He doesn't look like a ballplayer to me."

The thought that they might have someone as bad as the Wildcats' worst outfielder was a sobering one. But then Fenton shrugged.

"Oh, well. At least we don't have to face that for a while. Right now I'm just glad it's Saturday, and let's not waste any of it. You know what, Kerby?"

"What?"

"I wouldn't mind loosening up the old arm a little, just

to see how it feels." Fenton was the Panthers' star southpaw pitcher. "Let's play some catch!"

"Good idea! Come on, let's get our gloves!"

They sprang into action, but they had not made more than a spring or two before a commanding voice brought them to a stop.

"Hey, guys!"

Bumps hurried across the lot toward them. Their club president was built like a bully, big and chunky, and at one time he had been the terror of the neighborhood, as far as Kerby was concerned. But now they were friends.

"Hey, I just saw Pinky Marshall up on the corner and he said there's gonna be a hockey game, so let's grab our sticks and go over."

The suggestion met with instant approval. Hockey, any form of hockey, was their favorite winter sport. Ice hockey would have been their favorite if they could have gotten on ice somewhere, but rinks were few and far between in their city, and ponds seldom froze over hard enough. So they had to settle for street hockey, but that was fun, too.

Minutes later they were on their way. Kerby and Fenton were carrying standard street hockey sticks — plastic blades

bought at a local sporting goods store were fitted to wooden handles made for them by Kerby's father, who fancied himself as a carpenter and was actually pretty good at simple jobs like fitting handles to plastic hockey blades.

Bumps was carrying a stick that was similar but had a much larger blade. He was also carrying the equipment he used as the Panthers' catcher. Because of his size, he usually tended the net in hockey games. His mask, chest protector, and shin guards made a good substitute for a goaltender's regulation outfit.

He was also carrying a pair of mitts he had made for himself, and which looked a lot like the ones used by goalies such as Tony Esposito if you didn't look too closely.

"If Red shows up, I suppose we'll get another earful about that new kid I grabbed for the Panthers," said Bumps. "Aw, well, let him yap. Position is nine-tenths of the law."

"Possession," said Fenton, and added diplomatically, "but you're right, Bumps."

"Sure I am," agreed Bumps, and pointed ahead as they rounded a corner and Burnside Court came into view. "What did I tell you? There he is. Get ready for a lot of flak. And when the game starts, watch him for cross-checks and high-sticking and hooking and spearing and any other dirty trick he thinks he can get away with."

Burnside Court was a dead-end street, which made it a good place for hockey games. Two of the Wildcats lived there, so nobody complained too much about their games unless the noise got out of control. And not enough cars came or went to make a serious interruption in their game.

Several boys were passing a puck around in the middle of the street, including the Panthers' third baseman, Stevie Rizzo. All the others were wildcats. Eddie Mumford happened to glance around, and said, "Hey, here comes some more guys, now we can get a game going!"

Red Blake flipped the puck to Herm Schultz and straightened up for a look.

"If it ain't my old buddy, Bumps!"

"Now, don't start that again, Red!" growled Bumps, but Red surprised them by grinning. He waved a hand forgivingly.

"Aw, forget it," he said. "I've talked it over with some of the guys, and I guess they're right. No sense in splitting hairs about which side of the street that new kid lives on.

You needed him, and we didn't, and you couldn't even play us if you only had eight guys — so forget it."

"Huh?" Bumps was amazed. "Well, I'm glad your guys talked some sense into you!"

Kerby and Fenton exchanged a quick glance. They were more than amazed. They were suspicious. Under cover of the general conversation, they muttered their opinions to each other.

"I'll bet Red got a line on Louie from some kid that knew him in his old neighborhood," muttered Kerby.

"Yes, and I'll bet he's even worse than we think," muttered Fenton.

Meanwhile, Red was taking charge, as usual.

"Okay, let's see, we've got ten guys now. Pinky, let's you and me choose up sides. Clyde's playing goalie, and so is Bumps, so you take Clyde and I'll take Bumps."

This caused another knowing look to pass between Kerby and Fenton. Red Blake actually choosing Bumps to play on his side! Red was certainly going out of his way to make peace — and that was not like him.

"Okay," said Pinky, and tapped his next choice. "I'll take Claypool."

"Schultz," said Red.

"Rizzo."

"Carmichael."

"Maxwell."

"Mumford."

Eddie Mumford was one of the boys who lived in Burnside Court. His father had built a couple of goal cages for them, with chicken wire for netting. These were already set up in the street, and a board had been placed over the storm drain in the curb near the corner, the one place where a puck might be lost.

Pinky put Kerby at left wing, Fenton at right, and made Rizzo defenseman, with himself as center. Red also played center, with Schultz and Mumford as wings and Carmichael as defenseman.

Pinky and Red faced each other at a point that was more or less the same distance from each goal cage.

"Okay, Mumford and Maxwell, you take turns dropping the puck for face-offs," ordered Red, and that was the only rule that was made in the course of the game.

2

THEY HAD a good game.

There was lots of scoring and plenty of invigorating arguments, and when the game was over nobody was sure what the final score was and nobody cared. But everyone had scored at least once or twice, including the defensemen.

Once Kerby took a nice flip pass from Fenton and hit the corner on Bumps's stick side with a beauty. Another time Fenton deked Red and Eddie and then flipped a shot right between Bumps's legs. As for Red, he had scored twice with slap shots, which were his favorite. And the others had all had their moments, too.

But when the game stopped and they headed home for lunch, Kerby and Fenton went back to worrying.

"I'd like to know what's got into Red Blake," said Fenton.

"Yeh, he acted almost human," said Bumps. "It ain't normal."

Fenton told Bumps about their suspicions. A frown put heavy creases across their president's broad forehead. He slapped it with a meaty hand.

"Don't tell me we got ourselves our own Butterfingers Blatweiler, and that rat Red knows it!"

"That's our hunch," said Fenton. "I hope we're wrong, but . . ."

Bumps groaned.

"I'll bet that's it, all right! Well, the sooner we know what we're up against, the better." He took a look at the sunny sky, and proposed action. "Listen, with the weather like this, we could go over to the school field after lunch and — come on, let's go by Louie's house and tell him to meet us there. We might as well find out the worst now."

Louie Landowski was a skinny little kid who wore glasses. He didn't look as if he could see two feet in front of his nose, let alone follow the flight of a baseball. When they told him they were going to hit a few fungoes over at the school field and wanted him to come with them, Louie frowned uncertainly.

"Well, I have a lot of homework I want to finish first," he said, "but I'll be there as soon as I can."

As the three boys walked on home, Bumps was thoroughly disgusted, and more than a little discouraged.

"Any guy who sits inside and does homework on a day like this," he declared, "is gonna make a lousy left fielder!"

By the time they reached the school field after lunch, the weather was better than ever.

"We've played on colder days than this right in the middle of summer," Bumps remarked when they began to throw the ball around. "Remember the day we like to froze playing the Cougars?"

After they had played catch for a while, they took turns hitting. Then Fenton wanted to go out to the mound and throw a few pitches.

"Stand up at the plate with a bat to give me a target, Kerby," he said, and Kerby obliged.

"Okay, but no hard stuff, now, Fenton," said Bumps. "Limber up nice and easy. What with Louie Landowski and one thing and another, all we need is for you to get a glass arm and the Panthers are finished."

14

Fenton nodded, and threw a few easy pitches over the plate, while Kerby stood with his bat cocked and watched them go by.

But then Fenton sent one in that was fat and high, and it was too much for Kerby. He took a cut at it, and connected.

Kerby was no power hitter like Bumps, but this time he boomed one. It looked as if it might go all the way to the gully back of left field.

"Wow! Did that feel good!" he yelled.

"Ych, well, you can just go chase it!" ordered Bumps. But Kerby was in luck. As the ball soared high in the sky, a boy who had been walking on the sidewalk beside the field ran after it.

The ball was over his head, but he went back like a deer.

"Look at that guy go!" said Bumps, and then his eyes goggled.

The boy had leaped into the air and speared the ball barehanded. And all in the same flowing motion as he came down he whipped his arm around and threw.

The ball came in like a rocket, a perfect strike into Bumps's mitt at home plate.

Bumps looked at the ball in his mitt. He looked at the boy who was trotting in toward them. He looked at Fenton and Kerby.

"Did you see what I saw?" he asked them, and paused to get his words together. "That peg! Anyone who tried to come home would have been nailed by ten feet!"

"And how about that catch?" said Fenton.

"Bare-handed!" said Kerby.

The boy coming toward them was tall, well built, and black.

"Let's see you do that again!" said Bumps, when he reached the infield.

The boy grinned.

"Hit me a grounder," he said.

Kerby grabbed the ball from Bumps, swung the bat, and slammed a hot grounder in the general direction of third base. Actually, it was pretty well off the mark, over in the shortstop area. But the tall, dark stranger ranged over, scooped it up, and whipped a throw in to Bumps he didn't have to move to take.

"Hey!" said Bumps. "Do you catch *everything* that comes your way?"

16

The boy shook his head.

"No," he admitted, "I drop a couple every season."

"Every *season*?" cried Kerby, and his mouth stayed open. Dropping a couple of balls every *inning* was more like the Panthers' style — and the Wildcats'.

Bumps went to the heart of the matter.

"Yeh, but can you hit?"

"Sure, I can do pretty well with the stick."

"Kerby," said Bumps, "give him the stick."

Kerby handed him his bat. Bumps crouched behind the plate, winging the ball out to Fenton as he went down.

"Okay, Fenton," he said. "Show him a good one."

The boy grinned and stepped into the batter's box. Fenton wound up and threw him a curve, and it was a good one.

But not good enough.

CRACK!

Fenton's head slowly swiveled around as he joined his friends in watching the flight of the ball. It was quite a flight. Farther into the gully than even Bumps had ever hit one.

Fenton walked down from the mound to the plate.

"My name's Fenton," he said. "What's yours?"

The boy grinned again.

"Willie Mays," he said, and Fenton grinned, too, which was unusual for him.

"I can believe it," he said.

"No, I really mean it," said Willie. "My whole name is Willie Mays Whitford. My dad wanted to be a ballplayer, but he got hit in the leg in Vietnam. But he named us all after his special heroes, and that's how come I'm Willie Mays."

The key words came through loud and clear. They even struck Bumps.

"Us *all*?" he repeated. "You mean, there's more like you at home?"

"Sure. One of my brothers is named Hank Aaron Whitford, and my little brother is Bob Gibson Whitford. Not that he's so little," Willie added. "He's big for his age, and he's almost a better ballplayer than Hank or me."

Bumps's eyes rolled toward Fenton and Kerby and back to Willie. He was thinking about that other local team, the Cougars. Already they were threatening to become the team to beat. If the Whitford brothers had moved into Cougar

18

territory, then both the Panthers and the Wildcats could forget about playing baseball.

"Say, do you live around here?" asked Bumps.

"Not yet," said Willie, "but we're going to."

"Where?"

"Well, we're going to rent a house over on Pickett Avenue —"

Willie jumped as all three of his listeners yelled the same two words at once.

"Pickett Avenue?"

"Why, yes —"

"Where?" cried Kerby.

"Hey, listen —" began Bumps.

It took Fenton to ask the key question.

"The Flanagan house?"

Willie scratched his cheek.

"Flanagan? Yes, I believe that's the name of the people who used to live there —"

"Yeow!"

Willie Mays Whitford stared with surprise at the war dance that was going on around him. Suddenly Bumps stopped stamping around and grabbed Willie's shoulder.

"Happy day!" he cried. "Willie, we've got a ball team, and you're in our neighborhood, and you and Hank Aaron and Bob Gibson are gonna be on our team!"

Willie Mays obviously liked their enthusiasm. But his face fell regretfully.

"Hey, I wish I could," he said, "but when Dad was over talking to the real estate man we rented the house from, that man had a boy about my age. Dad and that boy got to talking baseball, and Dad told him we'd be glad to play on *his* team."

Willie's listeners stared at one another in a stunned silence. Then Fenton's lips moved, with difficulty.

"Red Blake's father is a real estate agent," he croaked.

"That's right, that's his name," agreed Willie, "Red Blake."

3

WILLIE LOOKED at his watch.

"Say, I got to get back. My dad's at the house with Mr. Blake, finding out about some things. I just walked over here to take a look at the school."

"But darn it all!" Bumps burst out. "You guys ought to be on *our* team!"

Willie shook his head sadly.

"I wish we could play on *both* teams," he said. "We all love to play. But when my dad says something, that's a contract, and he told Red we'd play with him. Well, I got to get moving. See you later!"

The boys nodded, and silently watched Willie walk away. Then Bumps tottered over and sat down on a players' bench on the sidelines. Again his meaty hand punished his broad forehead.

"Why did I have to grab that new kid?"

Kerby and Fenton were thinking the same thing, of course, but the damage was done.

"We can't let Red get away with this!" declared Bumps.

"What can we do?" said Kerby. "Red hasn't left us a leg to stand on!"

Even Fenton seemed to be at a loss.

"Between now and the start of the season," he declared grimly, "we'll just have to think of *something*."

A wry smile only made Fenton look grimmer as he pointed to another boy who was hurrying along the sidewalk toward them.

"Here comes our secret weapon."

Bumps took a look and ground his teeth.

"Louie! For two cents I'd twist his nose!"

"It's not his fault."

"He didn't have to move here, did he? He could have moved somewhere else, like New York, or China!"

With a heavy sigh Bumps came to his feet and picked up the bat and ball.

"Hold it right there, Louie!" he called. "Get over onto the field and let's see you catch a fly."

At least Louie had brought a fielder's glove with him, which was some encouragement. He put it on, trotted into the field behind third base, adjusted his glasses, and pounded his fist in his glove.

"Okay, let's see one!"

Bumps tossed up the ball, swung the bat, and hit a little pop fly straight out to him.

"I got it!" cried Louie, peering up into the sky. But then his early confidence began to ooze away. He blinked uncertainly, shuffled forward, then back . . .

"Watch out!" yelled Kerby, and Louie did the only sensible thing. He put his glove over his head and ducked. Even then the ball made quite a *chonk* as it bounced off a corner of his glove, and Louie collapsed on the turf.

The boy rushed out to him.

"You okay, Louie?"

He sat up and rubbed his head.

"Yes, I'm okay," he said bravely. "I lost it in the sun. Hit me another."

Bumps stared down at him, then turned to his friends with a look of reluctant admiration.

"Well, I gotta give him one thing," he declared. "The kid's all heart!"

Later in the afternoon an emergency meeting was being held back at the clubhouse.

The three two-legged members were sitting outside, even though the short February day was fading fast, and a chill was beginning to creep into the air. Waldo, however, being a stickler for routine, was sitting in his usual spot in the doorway.

"Well, Louie may be all heart," Bumps repeated, "but he's no Willie Mays."

"That's for sure. He may outhit Butterfingers Blatweiler and Moony Davis," said Kerby, mentioning the Wildcats' weakest batters, "but that's about all."

"And with three new superstars on his team, Red will bench them anyway, if I know him," said Fenton.

Bumps was in the depths of despair. "I tell you, I just don't see any way out of this."

Then he stared in the direction of the street and made a terrible noise deep in his throat.

Red Blake, accompanied by Pinky Marshall and Eddie

Mumford, was walking across the lot toward them in his cockiest manner. He waved a hand and grinned broadly.

"Hi, guys! What's new?"

Bumps scrambled to his feet, choking with rage.

"You stinker, you knew all about Willie Mays and his brothers when we were playing hockey this morning!"

Red stopped, hands on hips, to give his full attention to a nasty chuckle.

"I didn't start it, you did," he said. "You grabbed first, so when I got a chance I grabbed, too."

"Three for one! Is that fair?"

"Can I help it if I'm lucky?"

"Lucky my foot!"

Red threw up his hands.

"Okay, okay! Maybe I did get the best of it." He challenged Bumps with an arrogant stare. "You want to settle it fair and square?"

"You bet I do!"

"Okay, then. Tell you what we'll do. We'll play you for them."

"What?"

"You heard me. Hockey tomorrow, the Wildcats against

the Panthers. Of course, you've got to put up something, too, so we'll bet you the Whitford brothers against . . . well, against your clubhouse here," said Red, giving the nearest splintery board a contemptuous poke, "and if that isn't fair I don't know what is!"

Bumps stared around at Kerby and Fenton, then back at Red.

"What are you talking about?"

"I'm talking about a bet that will settle things! If you win, you get our new guys. If we win, your clubhouse belongs to us. Listen, how fair can I be? You've got to put up *something,* and this old shack is about all you've got. Of course, if you're going to turn chicken . . ."

Though his long face did not show it, Fenton was suffering. He knew from experience there was no stopping Bumps when he was aroused. He also knew from experience that Red Blake usually had something extra up his sleeve. But unfortunately Red knew Bumps well, too. He knew how mad Bumps could get, and when he was mad he was reckless.

Bumps was like a drowning man clutching at a straw. *Any* chance was better than none at all. His heavy jaw

27

jutted forward, his eyes flashed fire, and he took the bait.

"You're on!" he said. "It's a bet!"

Red stuck out his hand and Bumps grabbed it, and for a moment each tried to crush the other's fingers to a pulp. When this effort had ended in a draw, Red had more to say.

"Okay, it's a bet. Any Panther and any Wildcat is eligible to play, but we'll play with six guys at a time, like regular hockey teams. If more than six of your guys show up, you can substitute whenever you want to, and we'll do likewise, okay?"

"Okay!" cried Bumps, swept along by his passions. "We'll be there!"

"Two o'clock tomorrow, okay?"

"Okay!"

"We'll play till the church clock strikes three, okay?"

"Okay!"

"Good!"

Red grinned around at Pinky and Eddie and then turned back to Bumps.

"I've got my starting lineup all picked out. I'll be center, Clyde will be goalie, and Pinky will be a defenseman," he said, then added casually, "and if they can make it, Willie Mays and his brothers will fill in the other spots."

"*What?*"

With the air of someone who had expected an outburst, Red held up his hand.

"Take it easy! Don't forget, they're Wildcats now, just like Louie Landowski is a Panther, and they'll *stay* Wildcats till the game is over — and after that, too, if we win," Red added with a smirk. "So that's it, and if you want to use *your* new guy, go right ahead."

He glanced once again at their clubhouse, and loosed a parting shaft.

"I don't know yet what we'll do with this thing. Maybe we'll move it over into my backyard, or maybe we'll just bust it up and use it for campfires. We'll see you guys to tomorrow — unless you chicken out!"

4

WHEN RED and his buddies had strutted away, glancing back and snickering as long as they were in sight, Bumps leaned weakly against the lone tree that stood near their clubhouse.

"That sneaky bum! He oughta be a lawyer!"

Bumps stared at his friends with hollow eyes.

"Now we're really in a mess!" he said as indignantly as if someone else were responsible. "All we can hope for is that not enough of our guys show up to make a team — and that means at least four of our nine guys have to get sick by tomorrow!"

He brightened up pathetically at the thought.

"Hey, maybe this warm weather will bring on an epidemic!"

"It had better hurry," said Fenton grimly. But then he

shook his head. "Anyway, they'd never believe us. They'd say we chickened out. We've got to play."

Bumps's broad shoulders sagged.

"I guess so. There's no way out. Well, I'm gonna start calling the guys and see who can show up. Meeting's adjourned," said their president, and trudged away unhappily homeward.

His friends watched him go. Then they looked at their clubhouse and tried not to think about how terrible it would be to have it hauled away or broken up by Red and his buddies.

Next they looked around them at the long, dull shadows, which the sun, low in the west now and sinking behind a bank of gloomy clouds, was throwing across the turf of the vacant lot. Finally they looked at each other.

"If you ask me," said Fenton, "we've only got one hope left."

"That's right," said Kerby, "and let's hope she's there! How soon do you think? . . ."

"Well, at this time of year I'll bet she takes her constitutional early, because it will soon be getting dark," said Fenton. "So let's wait a while and then go over."

"I'm for it!" said Kerby. "The sooner we get help, the better!"

The place they were heading for was Peterson Park, a small, public park a few blocks away. It was there that Kerby had first met Mrs. Graymalkin.

Kerby and Waldo had been hurrying home through the park that afternoon when they saw a strange old lady standing near the drinking fountain.

She had the heel of her shoe caught in the drain. Kerby helped her work it loose, and for being so nice to her, she had given him an old chemistry set that had belonged to her own son, Felix, when he was a boy.

Since then, whenever they were in trouble, Kerby and Fenton had gone looking for her, with interesting results. Mrs. Graymalkin and the chemistry set had helped them out of some tough predicaments.

When they reached the corner across from the park, they were relieved to see a familiar antique car parked on the opposite side near one of the gates.

"There's Nostradamus!"

That was what she called her ancient sedan. Tall and

gaunt, with brass headlights and running boards and fenders that flapped like the wings of gooney birds when he was set in motion, Nostradamus was nevertheless surprisingly spry for his age.

"She must be in the park," said Kerby. "Let's go!"

Waldo had come along, of course. He always enjoyed a good run among the trees. When they had crossed the street he trotted over to give one of Nostradamus's rear wheels a friendly sniff, then tore off after the boys as they raced down the slope into the park.

The light was hazy now under the bare tree limbs, and there was a deepening chill in the air. Not even a squirrel was stirring among the dead leaves that carpeted the worn grass. The park seemed utterly deserted and still.

In short, conditions were perfect. Conditions were perfect for Mrs. Graymalkin to be enjoying one of her constitutionals, as she called the walks she took for exercise in the park.

With the trees and bushes bare it seemed as if they should have been able to spot her without any trouble, but for several minutes they walked this way and that without locating her. A sharp wind sent a swirl of dead leaves scurrying across the path in front of them, scraping the asphalt with tiny rustling sounds. Kerby shivered.

"It's getting cold," he said. "I'll bet you tomorrow's going to be another story."

"Good hockey weather," said Fenton with a gloomy grin that came and went quickly, as if surprised to find itself on his solemn face.

It was too cold to sit down on a bench to wait around, so they stood near the silent drinking fountain, turned off for the winter, and stamped their feet as the temperature seemed to be dropping degrees by the minute. To pass the time and take his mind off his shivering, Kerby needled Fenton about their strange friend.

"Well, you're always claiming she's not really a witch, but only a great scientist," he said, "but I hope you're wrong, because I'd hate to depend on plain old science to get us out of *this* mess!"

Here was one subject which Kerby could always count on to get a rise out of Fenton. Fenton was a strong believer in science. His back stiffened to ramrod straightness, and his eyes flashed.

"Oh, cut it out, will you, Kerby?" he snapped. "Just

34

name one thing she's ever done that can't be explained by science. One thing!"

"Well . . ."

"If she suddenly appeared in a puff of smoke, that might be different," said Fenton, "but —"

He had no chance to finish his statement, because just then a gust of wind howled through the park, a gust that took their breath away and lifted a whirlwind of dead leaves around them.

If left both boys with their eyes full of dust. And as they were rubbing them and trying to blink them open, they were startled to hear a familiar crackly voice.

"Mercy me, if it isn't Kerby and Fenton — and dear little Waldo! Whatever are you doing, lollygagging about in the park in this changeable weather? You'll catch your death of cold!"

Kerby gaped in astonishment. Mrs. Graymalkin was standing on the path in front of them, displaying her snaggletoothed smile.

He was glad to note she had foreseen the change in the weather and was wearing her heavy black cape, which was no less worn but certainly warmer than her lighter ones.

The enormous black feather that straggled from her large, black velvet hat danced a giddy pirouette and then settled down as the wind died away.

"Hello, Mrs. Graymalkin!" said Kerby. "We didn't know it was going to turn so cold, but we had to come looking for you, because we're really in a mess!"

Fenton seemed to have been badly shaken by the puff of wind and dust and dead leaves. He was still doing a good deal of blinking. Mrs. Graymalkin shot a sly glance down at him and treated them to an amused cackle that sounded like a dozen biddies in a barnyard after the rooster had told a good joke.

"Poor Fenton! You must learn to shut your eyes *quickly quickly quickly* when the wind brings us one of its surprises," she counseled. "So there is trouble afoot, is there?"

Fenton pulled himself together.

"There certainly is, Mrs. Graymalkin," he told her. "We need help, or we're going to lose our clubhouse —"

"And every baseball game we play the Wildcats!" added Kerby.

She peered down at them with twinkling eyes that were surrounded by a network of wrinkles.

"A mess? A mess? Oh, dear, oh, dear, not another one? I declare, it seems you boys simply cannot stay out of trouble!" She sighed, and stamped her ridiculously high-heeled shoes on the hard asphalt of the path as she said, "Well, what is it this time?"

Fenton told her all about Bumps and Louie Landowski and Red and the Whitford brothers.

"What interesting names!" she remarked. "Willie Mays and Hank Aaron and Bob Gibson!"

"They're all baseball stars," explained Fenton. "I mean, that's who they're named after."

"Oh, I see. Well, as you know, I'm not exactly up to the mark when it comes to our national pastime," said Mrs. Graymalkin. "However, I *do* know who their father is, because his picture has been in the newspapers and on television. He's always moving around for one of the government agencies. But go on. What happened next?"

Kerby told her about the bet Red had tricked Bumps into making.

"So you see, it's not our fault we're in this mess," he said. "Bumps made the bet."

Again the old eyes twinkled.

"Lackaday, lackaday — it's interesting how these messes you get into never seem to be your fault. Still, I must admit that in this case it would appear you are the innocent victims," she said. But then she frowned. "At the same time, I thoroughly disapprove of wagers."

"Wagers?"

"Betting, that is to say. And furthermore, as you know, I do not believe in helping anyone to gain an unfair advantage in *anything* in order to win."

"We know that," agreed Kerby unhappily. A good, helpful unfair advantage was exactly what they needed just then.

"Tell me," said Mrs. Graymalkin, "what would happen if your game ended in a tie?"

Kerby and Fenton stared at each other.

"Well," said Fenton, "I guess the bet would be off, and we would be right where we were when Bumps made the bet."

"Exactly where you should be," said Mrs. Graymalkin, nodding firm approval. "Yes, indeed — indeed, yes. Well, I'll see what I can think of to help you, but *only* if you promise to use my help to gain a tie, and no more."

Kerby and Fenton considered this with long faces. It was a hard bargain. They would still have to look forward to facing a Wildcat baseball team with three superstars added to it.

But at least they would still have their beloved clubhouse. Fenton faced the music for them.

"All right," he said, "we promise."

Mrs. Graymalkin nodded, and showed every other tooth — all she had left — in a smile.

"Very well!"

She laid a long, bony finger alongside her long, thin nose and closed her eyes.

"Now, let me see . . ."

5

THAT BONY index finger was what Kerby thought of as her thinking finger, because she always pressed it against her nose when she was thinking hard.

After a moment, as a rule, her eyes popped open, signaling the advent of one of her ideas.

This time, however, she opened one eye, and that one not very far.

"I do believe I need a bit more information concerning this game you're going to play, this hockey," she declared. "When I was young we used to play something quite similar, only we called it 'shinny.'"

"Shinny?" Kerby nodded. "I've heard my grandfather talk about shinny. He says it was just like our game except they made their own sticks."

"So did we," said Mrs. Graymalkin. "We girls used broomsticks with most of the broom cut off —"

"Broomsticks?" said Kerby, and darted a glance at Fenton as he repeated this suggestive word.

"That's right, broomsticks," she said. "And what do you call the thing you hit? . . ."

"The puck."

"Yes, yes, that's it, the puck. Well, our puck was likely to be anything we could find — a bone, a wad of black crepe sewed into a ball, or some small, dried-up thing — and we would fly back and forth between goals like mad, absolutely *fly,* and when too many opposing players caught up with us we would sometimes try to hit the puck to one of our teammates. And that is what I wanted to ask about. Do you hit the puck back and forth to each other in an effort to keep it away from your opponents?"

"Sure! We call that passing. We pass every chance we get," Kerby assured her. "Fenton and I even use a drop pass sometimes, and —"

"Do you indeed?" said Mrs. Graymalkin. "In that case, would it not be a distinct advantage if you could count on receiving the puck each time one of you attempted to hit it to the other?"

42

The boys would have rubbed their hands together, had they dared. Now Mrs. Graymalkin was talking business!

"Would it ever!" cried Kerby. "That would help plenty. Why, half the time somebody intercepts our passes."

"I can well believe it. As I remember, that certainly was the case in our shinny days — though to be sure, we had not then perfected the pass, to say the least. I'm afraid in general we tended to monopolize the puck as long as we could and make our goals singlehandedly," said Mrs. Graymalkin. "Well, now! With that information to work with, perhaps I can get somewhere!"

Once again she closed her eyes. And this time the boys did not have to wait long before they popped open.

"I have an idea," she said quietly, "but it will require unusual measures."

Fenton and Kerby were impressed. Her usual measures were unusual enough. What would unusual measures be?

"What do you mean, Mrs. Graymalkin?" asked Fenton.

"Well . . . Kerby, you still have that old chemistry set I gave you safely hidden away, I suppose?"

"Yes, ma'am!"

43

"Good, good, good. However, this time we shall have to unite the forces of chemistry with those of botany to achieve the desired results."

Fenton's cuphandle ears pricked up almost visibly at this exciting scientific news.

"Botany?" he repeated.

"Yes. Chemistry can cope with part of our task, but botany . . . however, we'll come to that later. First things first. Kerby's chemistry set can provide the sinistrodextrolic acid we need —"

"It can?" marveled Kerby.

"Yes, yes, yes — the third tube from the right, I should say. Simply look for SDA on the label. Using an eye-dropper, carefully let fall a single drop on the part of your stick you hit the puck with —"

"The face of the blade," said Fenton, who knew things like that.

"Is that what you call it, Fenton? Well, then. So much for chemistry — for the moment," said Mrs. Graymalkin briskly. "We have taken care of your sticks — but what about the puck? In order to make everything work out right, the puck must cooperate, too. And in order to co-

44

operate it must be rubbed with a special ingredient. That is why we must call upon botany. The puck must be rubbed with the tiny leaves of a rare herbaceous plant."

The big words were coming almost faster than Kerby could handle them, but he supposed that herbaceous had something to do with herbs.

"And do you know what that rare herbaceous plant is?" Mrs. Graymalkin went on to ask.

"No, ma'am," said Kerby. "What?"

The straggly black feather on her hat swooped dramatically as she threw back her head, and she raised a long, bony forefinger for emphasis.

"Wigglewort!" she cried.

The boys gaped at her.

"Wigglewort?"

"Wigglewort!"

Mrs. Graymalkin's eyes almost seemed to give off sparks as she pronounced the name.

"The wort family contains some of our most important plants, many of which have mysterious and even *magical* properties. There's adderwort and mulewort and mugwort and sneezewort, stitchwort, spleenwort, soapwort, spearwort, liverwort and glasswort, sawwort, throatwort and woundwort, bitterwort and butterwort, just to name a few," crooned Mrs. Graymalkin, glorying in the sound of them. "Adderwort, of course, is the common bistort, or snakeweed — but then, we mustn't let ourselves be swept away into a botany lesson, must we? No, no, no, not when there is still so much to do, so much to do!"

"I suppose not," said Fenton almost reluctantly — he had been listening with great interest. But now he asked eagerly, "Do you have some wigglewort we can use?"

"No," said Mrs. Graymalkin.

"Well, can you get some for us?" cried Kerby.

"No," said Mrs. Graymalkin.

"You can't? Then how —"

"Wigglewort," said Mrs. Graymalkin in portentous tones, "can be used effectively only by the person who finds it."

"What? You mean? . . ."

The boys exchanged helpless stares, and Kerby voiced the obvious drawback to this arrangement.

"But how can we find any wigglewort? We don't even know what it looks like!"

46

"Why, Kerby, dear, it's perfectly simple," said Mrs. Gray-malkin. "You merely look for a wort that wiggles."

"But I don't even know what a *plain* wort looks like!" Kerby insisted, and Fenton said, "Neither do I!"

Their friend sighed.

"Dear, dear, dear, the *natural* sciences are so neglected these days," she complained, shooting a sharp, twinkling glance at Fenton's glum face. "Well, fortunately, all the worts do *not* look alike — far, far from it!"

"They don't?"

"Certainly not! No one would confuse ragwort with mugwort — and as for bitterwort and butterwort, they're worlds apart — and *none* of them looks the least like wig-glewort, which glows in the dark and wiggles."

"Glows in the dark? And wiggles?" repeated Kerby. Now they had something to go by. "But where can we find any?"

Mrs. Graymalkin smiled her snaggletoothed smile and swept her hand around her in a wide circle.

"Everywhere! It grows everywhere! It's right here in this park!"

Kerby was dismayed. He looked at Fenton and saw a

boy who was having the same struggle believing what seemed to be a preposterous statement.

"I've certainly never seen a plant here in the park that glows and wiggles in the dark," said Fenton, "and we've been here at night."

"I know you have," said Mrs. Graymalkin. "I remember at least one occasion . . . Hallowe'en, I think it was? . . . But you must understand, wigglewort only glows and wiggles for those who can *see* it glow and wiggle. Actually, it was wrong of me to refer to it as a 'rare' plant. It is not so much rare as rarely *seen*. And in order to see it . . . well, that's where ophthalmesmerester comes in."

Kerby was staggered by the length of this latest arrival.

"That's where what-did-you-say comes in?"

"Ophthal — but don't worry about it, simply look for the tube labeled OME, about the fourth or fifth from the left," said Mrs. Graymalkin. "Just before you are ready to come back to the park to search for your wigglewort, drop two drops of OME into a beaker containing five cubic centimeters of water, and take a deep breath of the vapor."

"Two drops of OME . . . five cc's of water," muttered Fenton, making sure he had it straight.

"Exactly so! And as soon as you have breathed in the vapor, *run run run* straight to the park, and you will be able to see the dear little plant if you really search for it high and low, high and low, as round and round you go. Pluck only the first plant you find. Look no farther! Rub the puck with it — once, twice, thrice — any puck you use — and . . . well, I am sure you will find the results quite satisfactory, quite satisfactory!"

She paused for a squint at the darkening sky.

"I do hope you will be able to play your game tomorrow, though, for as the saying goes,

> *But for two-and-twenty hours*
> *Wigglewort retains its powers;*
> *Nothing darkest arts can do*
> *Will make it last past twenty-two!*

— which, on the whole, is a good thing," said Mrs. Graymalkin. "Otherwise, there might be abuses. And the time, by the way, is counted not from when you *find* your wigglewort, but from the moment when you first learn about it — so you have exactly twenty-two hours in which to find it and use it."

As she spoke, a bell tolled in the distance. It was the clock striking in the belfry of St. Swithin's Church, over near Burnside Court. It struck five times.

Fenton made a quick calculation, and caught his breath.

"Wow! That means it's only good till three o'clock tomorrow — and our game is going to start at two!"

"And end at three!" added Kerby.

"Gracious! Then it's fortunate we didn't meet any earlier," said Mrs. Graymalkin. "Well, now, you have a great deal to do, and as soon as you're ready and it is good and dark you must hurry back here to the park and begin your search — so off you go! *Run run run!*"

6

THERE WAS no one home at Kerby's house. His mother had left a note saying, "Gone shopping."

While Fenton ran home to fetch his hockey stick, Kerby took his from its place in the garage. With Waldo at his heels he hurried inside and down to the basement.

There he hauled out his chemistry set from its hiding place in his toy chest. Kerby kept it hidden there under a jumble of wooden blocks he had spent many happy hours playing with when he was younger.

He carried the chemistry set to his father's workbench and opened it. The inside of the lid was covered with printing in faded red and black letters:

FEATS O' MAGIC CHEMISTRY SET
Instructive! Entertaining!
Hours of Amusement!

Astonish Your Friends!
Entertain at Parties!
Make Extra Money Giving Demonstrations!

Lying in a row were corked glass tubes bearing faded labels. Another section of the box was full of eyedroppers, retorts, and beakers.

In a moment Fenton was back with his hockey stick. Together they scanned the tubes of chemicals in the box.

"First the sin — sin — whatever she called it," said Kerby. "Anyway, she said the third tube from the right, didn't she?"

"That's right. Sinistro . . . something or other, anyway SDA," said Fenton, "and here it is!"

He pointed to a tube. The lettering was blurred, but it unquestionably read "SDA."

Kerby uncorked it. Fenton chose an eyedropper and took a deep breath, bracing himself. He dipped the end of the eyedropper into the tube and sucked up a small amount of sinistrodextrolic acid.

"All right, let's see a stick," he said tensely.

Kerby corked the tube, put it back in its place, and

picked up his hockey stick. He held it up with the forehand side of the blade out flat. Fenton let a single drop of the chemical fall onto its surface.

There was a slight hiss, and a small puff of something like smoke, and that was all. Waldo, who had edged forward to watch, scampered back a few steps, but enjoyed the drama.

"Okay," said Fenton. By now beads of perspiration were shining on his sallow forehead. "Now my stick."

Kerby had to be sure to turn Fenton's stick the opposite way, because Fenton was left-handed. Again Fenton let a single drop fall onto the blade, and again the same hiss and puff resulted.

They both heaved a sigh of relief.

"Well, that's out of the way," said Fenton. "But what about the rest of it? We've got to wait till it's really dark, and that means we'll have to wait till after supper. And before we go over to the park, we've got to fix up that other stuff, that OME, and take a sniff of it so we can see the wigglewort."

"Yes, but after dinner my father might decide to come

54

down here and fool around at his workbench, and then where would we be?"

Fenton was looking at the chemistry set again.

"Here! Here's OME," he said, taking out a tube. "Listen, let's take the stuff we need and hide it over in my garage, where we can get at it after supper without having to worry."

"Good idea!"

"And bring the hockey sticks too, and a puck." Fenton was in high gear now, thinking hard and planning ahead. "We'll take them along."

"Why?"

Fenton frowned.

"Listen, if we do find any wigglewort, I want to know what it's going to do to the puck *before* we get into a game. However it works, we need to have a little practice session first."

"You're right, Fenton. Come on, let's get things squared away and hide the stuff before someone comes home and—"

Suddenly Kerby started so violently he dropped a hockey stick. It clattered on the floor, but not loudly enough to

drown out the ominous sound that had made him drop it
— the sound of a car in the driveway.

"There's Pop!"

Glassware tinkled in Fenton's trembling hands as he began madly putting things back into the box.

"Don't panic! Take it easy!" he cried in a panicky voice.
Then he caught hold of himself and began thinking again.
"You go on up and make sure they don't come down here.
I'll put this stuff away."

Waldo had already started up the stairs. Kerby raced up
behind him, and together they hurried outside. By then the
car was in the garage, and both his parents were getting out
of it.

"Hello, dear," said his mother. "How about some help
with the grocery bags? Your father came home early and
took me shopping, and we really loaded up."

"Good!" cried Kerby.

"Oh, are you hungry?"

"Er — sure!" said Kerby, though that was not the reason
he was delighted to see so many groceries. Here was just
what was needed to give Fenton some extra time.

"Were you down in the basement?" asked his father as

he handed a bag of groceries to Kerby. "I see the lights are on."

Kerby gulped and tried to keep his voice steady and innocent.

"Yeh, Fenton and I were fooling around," he said. "He's still down there."

They went inside to the kitchen. Waldo sat down beside Kerby to watch the groceries come out of the bags and see what brand of dog food would appear. Kerby and his parents were busying around when the basement door opened and Fenton joined them.

Fenton was carrying a small box, a box just about large enough to hold an eyedropper, a tube, and a beaker.

"Oh, hello, Mrs. Maxwell. Hello, Mr. Maxwell," he said in his usual polite way.

"Hi, Fenton!" said Mr. Maxwell. "How's everything?"

"Fine, thanks." Fenton glanced at Kerby and said, "Okay if I borrow this stuff, Kerby?"

"S-sure, Fenton," said Kerby.

And of course that was the time his father chose to take a friendly interest in the boys' doings.

"What have you got there, Fenton?" he asked brightly.

"WRO-O-OW!" yelped Waldo, and no one could blame him, because Kerby had stepped hard on his tail.

A general uproar resulted.

"Oh, gosh!" cried Kerby. "Waldo, why don't you watch where —"

"Listen, you know that dog has a tail!" lectured Mr. Maxwell. "Why don't *you* watch where you're going when he's around?"

Waldo raced away into the front of the house and Kerby hurried after him to apologize.

"I'm sorry, Waldo," he muttered, massaging his friend's tail, "but honest, it was in a good cause!"

Cautiously Waldo attempted a wag or two, and was relieved to find his tail would still work. Kerby was forgiven.

Fenton had recognized teamwork when he saw it. He was gone.

A few minutes later there was a knock on the back door. Fenton had returned.

"I forgot my hockey stick," he said. "Okay if I go get it?"

"Sure, Fenton, come in!" said Mr. Maxwell genially.

Kerby followed Fenton down into the cellar.

"I put the stuff in my garage," muttered Fenton. "Now how about grabbing your stick and a puck and let's try a few passes in your driveway? I want to see if anything happens yet."

"Okay!"

They went upstairs.

"Okay if we practice a little in the driveway, Mom?"

"Yes, but not too long, I'll have supper ready soon."

They hurried outside. Waldo, now fully recovered, came along.

It was good to relax.

"Wow!" said Kerby. "That was a close one!"

Fenton reached down to pat Waldo.

"Nice going, Waldo," he said. "Well, now, let's try the sticks."

They made a few sweep passes to each other. Nothing unusual happened.

"Might know it," said Fenton. "We'll have to find that wigglewort."

Waldo chased the puck back and forth, keeping out of the way, but snapping at it when it got past one of them and slowed down — he knew how hard the puck was, and that it was nothing to fool around with when it was traveling fast. Finally one shot went off into the grass and he was able to pick up the puck and bring it back to Kerby.

"Good boy," said Kerby. "Well, what do you say, Fenton? After supper we get together and . . ."

Fenton nodded. They put their equipment in the garage and Fenton ran home to get supper out of the way.

7

AFTER SUPPER the three met again in Kerby's driveway. It was pitch dark now, and colder than ever.

"Did you have any trouble getting out?" asked Fenton.

"No, but Mom said I can't stay long."

"Neither can I." Fenton uttered a short, grim laugh. "I
wonder what they'd think if they knew we were going over
to the park to look for some crazy thing called wigglewort?"

They took their sticks and the puck from Kerby's garage
and headed for Fenton's. This involved pushing aside a
loose board in Kerby's back fence, slipping through, and
crossing a corner of the vacant lot into Fenton's backyard.

Fenton hurried into the garage and came out with the
small box he had brought over from Kerby's basement. He
had already taken out the beaker. He handed the box to
Kerby.

"Here, hold this stuff. I'll go in and get the water."

Fenton tiptoed up the back steps and into his house, making no unnecessary noise whatsoever. But then, while Kerby stood around outside in the cold and the dark, it seemed to him that Fenton was taking forever. As usual, he tortured himself with visions of instant disaster. He pictured Fenton's father suddenly appearing in the kitchen and . . .

"Well! What are you doing here, Fenton? I thought you went over to Kerby's house. And what is that you are hiding behind your back in such a guilty manner? Ah-ha — a glass beaker! With water in it! What, pray tell, is going on here? Now, you just march over here and show me exactly what you were intending to do with that at this hour of the night —"

The back door opened. Fenton closed it quietly behind him and came down the steps.

"Where have you been? Anybody see you?"

"No. They were all in watching television."

"What took you so long?"

"I decided I'd better grab a sandwich bag. If we do find that wigglewort, we need something to put it in."

Kerby relaxed, and shook his head admiringly.

"Fenton, you sure think of everything."

"Ha!" said Fenton glumly. "If I thought of everything soon enough, we wouldn't be in this mess. Come on, let's put the two drops of that OME in this and see what happens. Hold the beaker, and I'll do it."

They moved around to the side of the house, where there was just enough light to see by. Kerby took the beaker and gave Fenton the box. Fenton uncorked the tube of OME and used the eyedropper. Then he squeezed two drops of the chemical into the beaker.

Sizzzz!

A cloud of vapor rose above the neck of the beaker, startling them both, but Fenton had presence of mind enough to say, "Sniff!"

They both sniffed. The smell was faintly pungent, but not unpleasant.

"Come on, let's get out of the light," said Fenton nervously. "If anyone saw us they'd think we were sniffing glue or something!"

He put the tube and eyedropper back in the box. Kerby held up the beaker.

"What shall we do with this stuff, Fenton?"

"Dump it out. I hope it doesn't kill the grass!"

Kerby emptied the beaker on the ground, then put it in the box, which Fenton hid in a corner of the garage.

"Okay, let's go!"

Waldo was sniffing curiously at the spot where Kerby had emptied the beaker.

"Here, let that alone!" ordered Kerby.

Glancing around uneasily, they skulked across the vacant lot and ran down the street toward the park.

Once they were inside the park they slowed down. For one thing, it was so dark on the silent paths they could hardly see where they were going.

"Where shall we start looking?" wondered Kerby, as if their eyes were not already darting around in every direction. They were almost as afraid of seeing something strange as of not seeing it.

"Let's walk up to Indian Rock. That's the spookiest part of the park," said Fenton. "If there's a wigglewort anywhere, it ought to be there."

"Good idea." Kerby tried to sound enthusiastic, but a shiver ran down his spine at the thought. Indian Rock was a large rock ledge at the far end of the park. The local legend was that Indians used to sacrifice their victims on top of the rock. Nobody really believed it, but it was the sort of legend that was easier not to believe in the daytime than it was in the dark.

"That other time we walked up there at night, it wasn't scary at all," Fenton reminded Kerby, and managed to chuckle feebly as he added, "Besides, we have Waldo to protect us."

The idea of Waldo protecting them was so funny it made Kerby laugh too, and laughing gave him courage.

"Besides that, we're armed. We've got our hockey sticks!"

They picked their way along the gloomy paths and then turned into the thick woods that filled the far end of the park. Soon the rocky ledge loomed up vaguely ahead of them.

"Keep your eyes peeled," muttered Fenton, "and remember, the first one of us who sees any wigglewort has got to pick it and be the one who rubs it on the puck."

They always did their best to follow Mrs. Graymalkin's instructions to the letter.

"Okay," said Kerby, but secretly he was hoping he would

not be the one who found it. Somehow he did not care for the idea of picking a plant that glowed and wiggled.

They had begun looking around near the base of the ledge when all at once Waldo barked. The sound made both boys jump.

"Cut it out, Waldo!" cried Kerby. "You want to scare somebody to death?"

Waldo was whining and woofing, darting forward and jumping back.

"Look!" said Fenton.

They dropped their hockey sticks and went to their knees beside Waldo. There, near a twisted tree trunk, something was shining in the dark.

"He's found some!"

"He took a sniff of that stuff I poured out!"

The pale, greenish, spectral light they were clustered around made Kerby think of about twenty lightning bugs all glimmering at once. Fenton dared to lean down for a closer look.

"It's glowing!"

"And it's wiggling!"

"Then it must be . . ."

66

"It's got to be . . ."

"Wigglewort!"

They stared at each other in great consternation.

"What are we going to do now?" asked Fenton. *"Waldo* found it! But *he* can't pick it and rub it on the puck, so —"

"Waldo, why can't you mind your own business?" demanded Kerby. "Now look what you've done!"

"Hey!" said Fenton excitedly. "Here's some more!"

He had spotted another small plant on the other side of the tree.

"But Mrs. Graymalkin said to pluck the first plant we found, Fenton!"

"Well, she meant you and me."

"Waldo was there when she said it."

They argued the point anxiously for a while without getting anywhere.

"Listen, we've just got to take a chance," said Fenton. "I'm *sure* we'd be wrong to pick Waldo's, so that leaves mine, and I'm going to pick it."

"Well . . . I guess that's all we can do now."

Still on his knees, Kerby moved over next to Fenton, and

68

they stared down at their mysterious quarry. Fenton rubbed a trembling hand up and down the side of his slacks.

"Go ahead," urged Kerby. "Pick it!"

"Don't rush me!"

"Well, we haven't got all night," said Kerby, though he well knew the act of touching the small, glowing, wiggling plant was one that took some courage.

Fenton reached down gingerly, took hold of it, and plucked it hastily from the earth.

8

"GOT IT!" cried Fenton.

"Hey!" said Kerby. "It's stopped glowing!"

"Yes," said Fenton, "and stopped wiggling, too."

"Maybe it shouldn't," said Kerby. "Maybe that shows we picked the wrong one."

"We'll soon find out."

"Where shall we go?"

"The tennis court."

The park's one tennis court had a streetlamp beside it. Since the net had been taken down for the winter, the surface was clear, making it an ideal place for them to try a few passes.

Seen by the light of the streetlamp, the wigglewort in Fenton's hand looked like the commonest sort of little weed.

"Okay, let's have the puck," said Fenton.

Kerby handed it over.

"Now, remember how Mrs. Graymalkin moved her hand when she told us how to rub the puck?"

"Sure." Kerby imitated the movement. "Back and forth, real fast, once, twice, thrice."

"Right. So that's the way I'll do it."

Rubbing the puck briskly, Fenton chanted, "Once, twice, thrice!"

He almost dropped it, because for an instant it seemed to glow in his hand.

"My gosh, Fenton! Would you look at that!"

"It works! Here, Kerby, you take it!"

"Me?"

"Yes! Come on, I want to put away our wigglewort," said Fenton, his voice throbbing with excitement and new-born confidence.

Kerby suffered an attack of gooseflesh, but forced himself to take the puck. He half expected it to quiver in his hand, but it didn't. It was not glowing any more, either. It felt perfectly normal. Fenton stowed the sandwich bag with its precious contents in his pocket. Picking up his hockey stick, he walked across the tennis court and faced Kerby.

"All right, drop it and shoot me a pass."

Kerby dropped the puck, squared away, and sent a sweep pass to Fenton. It slid across the hard-surfaced court to him straight as a die. Fenton sent one back that was just as true.

"Okay, now, let's start moving around a little."

They began to shoot passes to each other on the run, and every pass was a beauty. Before long they were trying some pretty fancy stickhandling, still without missing a pass.

"Great! Now for a goal!" said Fenton, and swept a shot at the netting along the back of the court.

The puck started toward the net, then veered to the left and slid in a wide circle back to Kerby!

Kerby slammed it at the net, but again it veered away and slid back — to Fenton!

They stopped and stared at each other, dismayed.

"For Pete's sake, what good are passes if we can't make a goal?" cried Kerby.

Then Fenton brightened up.

"I know!" he said, and shot a pass over to Kerby. "Hit me another one."

Kerby sent a sweep pass back to Fenton — and Fenton tried a backhand shot.

72

Zing! went the puck, straight into the net. Fenton threw up his arms as if he had scored an actual goal.

"You see? When we don't want to hit it to each other, we have to use the *back* side of the blade, the side we didn't put any SDA on!"

After that everything looked better and better. No matter how they hit their forehand shots, the puck curved from one stick to the other. But when they tried a backhand shot it went straight.

Waldo frisked around, chasing the puck, but never got anywhere near it. After a while, when they stopped to rest, he flopped down on the court, panting. Fenton was behind him just then with the puck.

"Hey, Kerby, move over so Waldo's right between us," he said. "I've got an idea."

Kerby moved over. Fenton hit one straight at Waldo, but not hard enough to hurt him if it hit him.

When the puck was two inches from Waldo's tail, it zipped sideways, curved around him, and went on to Kerby.

Waldo leaped to his feet, startled to see the puck whisk past so close. Kerby hit it straight back at him. Waldo

pounced at it — but it curved past his nose and swerved around him back to Fenton's stick.

As he stared down at the puck, Fenton was in the grip of strong emotion. Patting his pocket where the sandwich bag was, he said hoarsely, "Kerby, did you see what I saw? The Bruins or the Rangers or the Canadiens — any of them would give a million dollars for it! No matter how many guys are in the way, every time we pass the puck at each other, it's going to get there!"

Fenton picked up the puck.

"We'd better get home before somebody misses us," he said. "I don't care *who* Red Blake has on his team tomorrow, we're ready for him!"

9

WINTER was back on the job. When Kerby and Fenton met out in front of the clubhouse the next afternoon, it was bitter cold. A blustery wind made their eyes water and their breath steam.

"Have you got the wigglewort?" asked Kerby.

Fenton patted the pocket of his heavy jacket.

"Right here."

"What if somebody sees you rub the puck with it?"

"Don't worry about that. The first chance I get to chase it when it goes out-of-bounds over the curb I'll pick it up with my back turned, and it will look like I'm just brushing something off of it. After that, be sure not to hit any fore-hand shots unless you're passing to me."

After all, if they pulled off too many passes, Red might start to get suspicious.

"Use your backhand most of the time, and so will I," said Fenton, "but watch for the big chances."

They walked over to Bumps's house and yelled for him a few times. Presently he came out carrying his equipment. He gave the sky a disappointed glare.

"I was hoping for a couple of feet of snow," he told them. "This is one game I ain't looking forward to."

"Who else did you get for our side?"

"Bingo Klotz for center, and Stern and Rizzo for defensemen." Bumps shrugged. "We could do worse. We'll just have to see how good those Whitford guys really are, that's all."

Fenton's face remained solemn, but his eyes had a strange twinkle.

"Well," he said, "I'm ready to give it that extra little bit."

"So am I," said Kerby, trying not to grin. "They'll know they're in a game!"

Their confident tone perked up Bumps a bit.

"They won't put any shots past me without a fight!" he assured them.

When they reached Burnside Court their spirits improved still more. The street was full of hockey players, in-

77

WASHINGTON TOWNSHIP ELEMENTARY SCHOOL LIBRARY

cluding their three Panther teammates and at least seven Wildcats, but there were no Whitford brothers to be seen, and Red Blake was trying to look unconcerned.

"Where's Willie Mays?" asked Bumps.

"Don't worry, he'll be here. They'll *all* be here!" blustered Red.

"Then why aren't they here now?"

Over in the next block St. Swithin's clock struck twice. Fenton held up his hand.

"Hear that? You said we'd start playing at two o'clock —"

"And you've already got plenty of guys here," added Kerby, "more than you need."

Bumps jerked a thumb in Red's direction and sneered his mightiest sneer.

"Maybe he's too chicken to play us with his regular guys . . ."

That did it, of course.

"Nobody's chicken!" snarled Red. "We'll start playing you any time you want to!"

"Like right now?"

"Okay!"

Red turned and waved to the others.

78

"Come on, you guys, let's get organized. Now, listen," he said as they all gathered around, "we'll play till the clock strikes three, and whoever is ahead then wins, okay?"

"Okay!"

Red went on talking for a while, making a few more special rules for so important a game, and it suddenly occurred to Kerby that right now, while everybody else was busy listening to Red, would be a good time for —

Fenton thought so, too. When Kerby glanced around, looking for him, he was just in time to see Fenton's hand brush back and forth briskly, once, twice, thrice, over the surface of the puck he was cupping in his hand.

As soon as he had finished he dropped the puck and moved around the edge of the group until he was standing on the opposite side from Kerby. As he did so, he glanced across at Kerby and nodded.

This time when he had rubbed it with the wigglewort the puck had not glowed. But Kerby reminded himself it was not dark enough now to see any glow, even if they still could have. At the same time he could not help but worry for fear the wigglewort had lost its stuff.

Stepping back to where Fenton had dropped the puck,

Kerby gave it a little tap. He watched it slide in a wide curve around the group till it came to rest against the blade of Fenton's stick. They exchanged another glance, and a grin came and went swiftly on Fenton's solemn face.

"Hot diggety!" breathed Kerby.

They were in business.

The same as the day before, Kerby and Eddie Mumford took turns dropping the puck for face-offs. Red won the first face-off from Bingo, scooping the puck sideways to Eddie who passed to the other wing, Pinky Marshall, but Fenton's sweep check took it away from Pinky and Fenton got off a flip pass in the general direction of the other side of the street.

There were a lot of feet and sticks in its path, but the puck wigglewaggled this way and that and went clear across to Kerby, who sent a forehand sweep straight toward the Wildcats' goalie, Clyde Marshall.

Clyde was all set for it, ready to block it with his big goalie's stick, but before it ever got near Clyde it took a crazy sort of bounce off to the side toward Fenton, who was running in at an angle. Fenton deked Clyde by switching suddenly to a backhand shot and the puck flipped past Clyde's gloved hand for a goal.

Naturally all the Panthers had to cheer and hug Fenton and each other after scoring, just like the hockey teams did on television. Then, when they broke up to go to their positions for the next face-off, Fenton was able to mutter to Kerby, "Okay, now backhand."

This was the strategy they had agreed upon. Make a goal, then avoid passing to each other till the Wildcats evened the score.

"It isn't going to be easy to end up with a tie," Kerby had pointed out, "but if we do all we can to make sure, then at least Mrs. Graymalkin can't blame *us* if something goes wrong and we accidentally end up a goal ahead."

Even Fenton, as hopelessly fair and square as he tended to be, was forced to agree with this, and Kerby squirmed guiltily but with secret delight at his own innermost thoughts, one of which was:

Wouldn't it be great if — accidentally, of course — we *did* win!

82

The game was on again, and Red Blake was hogging the puck, trying to bull his way past everybody and score. Stevie Rizzo hooked it away from him as Red was coming down the left side of the street, but then Stevie got rid of it by shooting a pass over toward the other defenseman, Tommy Stern.

It never reached him. Pinky Marshall picked it off squarely in front of the crease and slammed it past Bumps into the net.

"Stevie, you bum!" yelled Bumps, while the Wildcats went through the leaping and hugging routine, "how many times have you got to hear it — never pass across in front of your own net!"

At that painful moment a new arrival came running into Burnside Court carrying a hockey stick. The small boy was wearing glasses and an earnest expression.

"Hi, guys! Can I play?"

Bumps's head swiveled around and he sizzled a stare at the newcomer.

"Louie!"

Bumps's expression clearly showed the conflict of emotions that was going on inside him. Here was the boy who had started all the trouble.

It would have relieved Bumps's feelings greatly to twist Louie Landowski's nose then and there for having moved into the neighborhood — or rather for having *not quite* moved into the neighborhood, which was the real source of trouble.

Yet as Fenton had pointed out, they could not really blame Louie.

Furthermore, there was that bonehead play that had just taken place . . .

"Can I play?" repeated Louie.

"Stick around," growled Bumps, and shot a thunderbolt glance at his delinquent defenseman. "I may put you in for Rizzo!"

10

THE NEXT face-off was a wild scramble, with the puck finally going to Pinky, who broke away and got off a flip shot from a good angle. All the time Bumps was yammering away in the crease, because goalies are supposed to keep up a string of chatter.

"Stay with him, Bingo, stay with him — keep it going, keep it going — Aw, no you don't! Watch yourself! Hey hey — Got it!" he yelled, and made a good catch of the puck. He tossed it to Tommy Stern, who worked it around Eddie Mumford and got off a short pass to Kerby.

Kerby had two Wildcats on him and couldn't see where Fenton was, but he took a healthy swipe at the puck and left the rest to Mrs. Graymalkin's recipe. As soon as he got the puck away he was free, with the two Wildcats racing away after it, so he headed for their goal.

Now he could see where Fenton was, up ahead, and sure enough the puck was bouncing around but heading his way. Fenton wasted no time hitting it a lick, and back it came in a crazy zigzag to Kerby. Clyde had already made a move in the wrong direction, and Kerby's backhand was past him before he could get back.

The score was two to one.

Again Kerby and Fenton relaxed, ready to let the Wildcats even the score. For a while, however, both goalies made some nice saves and nobody scored. But then Bingo Klotz had a chance at a screen shot that was a setup, and he put it past Clyde.

Now the score was three to one.

"Well, it's nice to have a little margin," Kerby murmured to Fenton. And as if to prove his point a car stopped at the head of the street and a voice called, "Tommy!"

Tommy Stern looked around with great reluctance.

"Yeh, what is it, Mom?"

"You've got to come home right away, your Uncle Morris and Aunt Sadie are here!"

"Aw, gee, do I have to?"

"Tommy, right this minute!"

86

Tommy groaned, looked around, said, "Gee, I'm sorry, guys," and trudged away to the family car. Red Blake turned to Bumps with a needling grin and looked over at Louie Landowski, waiting eagerly on the sidelines.

"Well, I guess this is when we get to see your new star!" he said.

Bumps glared, unable to hide his dismay. Tommy was their best defenseman. And now he had no choice but to beckon to his lone substitute.

"Come on, Louie!"

Louie's small face brightened and glowed with the light of battle as he jumped out onto the chilly asphalt, and play resumed. For a while there was a general scramble. Then Kerby, hard-pressed but not wanting to pass to Fenton when they were two goals ahead, backhanded the puck to Louie.

Red happened to be the Wildcat closest to Louie at that instant. He decided here was a good opportunity to swarm all over the newcomer and show him who was boss.

"Hey! Come on, let's have it!" he yelled, rushing at Louie.

Red had never been more surprised. Because little Louie

swung around and caught him with a beautiful hip check that all but sent him on his ear, and took off with the puck in a display of stickhandling that caught everyone flat-footed. It took the other Wildcats a second or two to react, and that was more time than they could afford, because by then Louie was sending a wrist shot right between Clyde's legs. Clyde tried to drop on it, but was a split second too late.

Now the score was *four* to one!

"Time-out! Each side gets a couple of time-outs!" yelled Red, making up a new rule. He glared at the Panthers as they gave Louie the hero's treatment. "This is no fair! He's a regular ringer!"

"Baloney!" yelled Bumps. "We didn't know he was worth a darn! I didn't even put him in till I had to, did I?"

"Anyway, what about *your* ringers?" said Fenton. "You were going to use the Whitfords —"

"Yeh, where are they?" jeered Bumps.

"Don't you worry!" said Red, looking worried enough for everybody, "they'll be here soon, and when they do get here, look out!"

88

"Be glad to see 'em," said Bumps. "Don't forget, they'll soon be Panthers!"

The game continued, and the Wildcats were failing to close the gap. They scored several times — mostly Red and Pinky — but so did the Panthers. Even with Fenton and Kerby trying *not* to pass to each other and *not* to score, the Panthers did all right. Bingo Klotz scored twice more, and Stevie and Louie once apiece. With about fifteen minutes left to play, the Panthers were still three goals ahead.

"Well, Mrs. Graymalkin can't say *we* won the game," Kerby muttered worriedly to Fenton after Bingo had made it eight to five.

"I hope *she* sees it that way," muttered Fenton just as worriedly. Neither of them wanted to save their clubhouse and win the Whitfords at the price of losing her friendship.

They took their places for the face-off. The puck came to Kerby, and Red and Eddie Mumford ran at him from two directions. The three of them managed to get feet and arms and sticks mixed together in one grand tangle, and all three of them went sprawling.

They were all up in an instant, grabbing sticks and running to join the battle over where Louie was trying to take the puck away from Bruce Carmichael near the Panthers' goal.

Red got it and sent a slap shot toward Bumps that looked like a sure goal. But instead of traveling straight it swerved wildly in the air and Fenton had it, clear over on the other side of the street.

Fenton made a rush for the Wildcats' goal and pushed a forehand at Pinkie, expecting to see it get past him to Kerby, but his angle seemed to be all off, because it curved away and slid back up the street to Red.

"Eddie!" yelled Red, seeing Eddie Mumford in the clear, and shot a pass his way — but it rolled in a horseshoe curve back to Fenton instead, who tried a sweep pass to Kerby, only to see the puck go to Red, who tried another shot at the goal, only to see Fenton get the puck before it ever reached the net —

"Aw, nuts!" yelled Red in frustration, and banged his stick hard on the pavement.

Crack! Its shaft snapped. Red looked down at it and

90

shouted, "Time-out! I got the wrong stick! This ain't mine!"

He glanced around, and grabbed Eddie Mumford's. "*You* got mine!"

Eddie stared around, and before he even grabbed for it, Kerby knew whose stick he was going to grab.

When they had taken that tumble they had all picked up the wrong sticks. As he looked down at the one he was holding, Kerby knew at once it was not his.

"Hey, you got mine, Kerby!" said Eddie, and Kerby let him have his.

"Then you busted Kerby's," Bumps told Red. "What did you have to do that for?"

"Aw, I only busted the shaft," said Red. "The blade's still okay, so stop squawking!"

He turned to a Wildcat who had been on the sidelines for the whole game, poor Butterfingers Blatweiler.

"Hey, Butterfingers, let Kerby use your stick, so we can finish the game."

"Okay — but if you bust it you got to buy me a new one," Butterfingers told Kerby.

Kerby glanced at Fenton and saw he looked almost cheerful. Now they would not be able to get off any more trick passes, but with a three-goal lead and their side playing as well as they were, they didn't need to. Less than fifteen minutes to go . . . it was a cinch!

Or at least so it seemed, except that before they had lined up for the next face-off a car pulled up at the head of the street and two boys got out. They had hockey sticks with them.

"Hi, guys!" called Willie Mays Whitford. "We too late to get a piece of the action?"

11

THE CAR rolled away. Besides the man who was driving, there was still one boy in it.

"This is Hank Aaron," said Willie, waving a hand at his brother.

Red Blake's face had lighted up, but he glanced around greedily.

"Where's Bob Gibson?"

"He's got a cold, so Mom let him ride over with us but she said he can't play. Dad has to go over and see your father about something," Willie told Red, "and he said for us to meet him there after the game is over."

Red continued to look as if Christmas had come early. Two out of three wasn't bad. He wasted no time putting those two to use.

"Willie, you go in for Mumford," he said. "Hank, you go in for Carmichael. Okay, now we'll see what's what!"

93

Off to one side, Kerby and Fenton were staring at each other in a wild state of alarm. Now what could they do? They didn't have their secret weapon any more. They would not be able to keep the puck away from Willie and Hank by passing it to each other. Their only hope was that the Whitfords would not be as good at hockey as Willie was at baseball.

That hope did not last long. Bingo won the face-off from Red and got the puck to Kerby, but Willie was right there and stole it from him with a hook check before Kerby knew what was going on.

The rest was murder.

Willie and Hank each seemed to know where the other was every minute. They kept the puck humming back and forth so fast it was almost impossible to get it away from them.

Bumps made two great saves, but even so the score had soon moved from eight to five to eight-all on two goals by Willie and one by Hank. With less than five minutes left to play, the score was tied, and Red was looking almost as pleased with himself as if he had scored the goals personally.

"Okay, we need one more!" he yelled. "Let's go!"

94

This time everybody was in there playing his very best, but even so, after a while Hank got the puck and he and Willie pulled a real razzle-dazzle. When it was over Bumps was flat out in the crease and the puck was in the net and the score was nine to eight.

The Wildcats made a big production of the leaping and hugging routine — after all, it used up time — but Bumps was wise to that and yelled, "Come on, knock it off and play!"

With heavy hearts the Panthers lined up for what might well be the last face-off of the game. And none of their hearts weighed any heavier than Kerby's and Fenton's. Kerby felt as if he had that whole huge clock over in St. Swithin's belfry ticking away in his head like a time bomb, ready to go off any second.

By now Red was so cocky he was a little careless, and Bingo won the face-off. He flipped the puck to Fenton. Before Pinky and Hank could get it away from him Fenton stabbed it desperately to Louie Landowski. And Louie, to everybody's amazement, somehow deked his way around Willie and slapped the puck down the street ahead of Kerby.

Nobody expected to see the puck in Wildcat territory anymore. Clyde Marshall had practically gone to sleep in front of his goal — in fact, he had wandered forward to watch the action and was two steps farther from the net than he had any business being when Kerby suddenly caught up with the puck.

With his eye on the goalmouth Kerby swept his blade at the disc and caught it square and true. Clyde made a dive for it, but too late. Chicken wire twanged as the puck bounced around inside the net, and the church clock applauded once, twice, thrice —

"Bong! Bong! Bong!"

Louie and Kerby took quite a pounding from their teammates and did not mind it at all.

But then Red Blake had to spoil everything.

"Okay, okay, you tied the score!" he yelled. "Now we go to sudden death!"

And Bumps, fired up and ready for anything, echoed the fatal words.

"Okay — sudden death!"

A sudden death play-off! That meant playing until one team scored another goal — and that team won!

Kerby stared at Fenton. He saw a tall, pale boy who looked ready to throw himself down on the cold asphalt and give up the ghost.

Just when they were safe, just when they were in the clear, Bumps had done it again!

They had scored one goal against Willie and Hank, but the chances of doing it again before one of those two scored were about a hundred to one. Or zilch, zero.

Kerby started to ask Fenton what they could do, but decided it was a waste of time. There was nothing they could do.

"Come on, let's go!" yelled Red, eager to finish the game.

Kerby and Fenton were dragging themselves to their positions when a car came wheeling around the corner and squealed to a fender-flapping stop behind the Panthers' goal.

It was a strange car, a real antique, a tall and narrow old sedan, with a funny-looking old lady at the wheel.

She stuck her head out the window and screeched in a

scratchy voice, "Oh, dear, oh, dear, oh, dear! This can't be the right street. Young man! You!" she called, pointing at Fenton, "would you give me directions, please?"

For an instant Fenton froze, too amazed to move. Then he unfroze.

"Time-out!" he yelled, and ran to the ancient sedan.

While Fenton talked to the driver Kerby held his breath. And Red Blake, for one, quickly became impatient.

"Come on, Fenton, you're holding up the game!"

Everybody else was yelling. Only Kerby kept his eyes on Fenton and the car, so nobody else noticed how Mrs. Graymalkin snapped her fingers above Fenton's head, and how a puff of smoke seemed to come and go almost before you could see it. Then Fenton turned and ran to his position, and the ancient sedan backed out of the street and rattled away.

"Old nuts like that oughtn't to be driving!" said Red Blake. "Okay, let's go!"

Red won the face-off and shot the puck toward Willie. Willie passed to Hank, but at that point Fenton flashed into the play, and Hank never got his stick on the puck.

Everyone but the goalies seemed to be involved in the

98

scramble that surrounded him, but Fenton was a tiger. When Willie got the puck again and slammed a shot at the Panthers' net that looked like a sure thing, it was Fenton's blade that picked it off in midair and somehow kept control of it right on down the street.

Red, Herm Schultz, and both Whitfords were all trying to take the puck away from him, but Fenton gave an exhibition of stickhandling that would have left the Boston Bruins with their tongues hanging out.

A tornado of sticks, arms, elbows, legs, knees, and feet moved down the street toward the Wildcats' goal, until suddenly Fenton snapped off a shot at the corner of the goalmouth that bounced off Clyde's glove — and into the net!

"We win!" screamed Kerby. "The Panthers win!"

100

12

BY THE TIME the Panthers had finished jumping up and down and hugging each other, Red Blake had already headed for home, followed by the rest of the Wildcats. When Willie and Hank started to leave, too, however, Bumps grabbed their arms.

"Wait a minute! We'll *all* walk over with you!" he said. "Don't forget, you're Panthers now!"

And besides that, of course, walking by Red's house would give them an extra chance to needle the Wildcats' captain.

"Well . . ." Willie glanced at Hank, and then grinned at Fenton. "Man, that was some of the slickest stickhandling I ever expect to see!"

"I was playing over my head," said Fenton modestly.

When the procession started off for Red's house, Kerby

had a chance to drop back and ask Fenton a few burning questions in private.

"What did she say? What did she do?"

"I still don't get it," said Fenton, puzzled. "She said, 'I've just heard something that makes it all right for you to win, so go back there and win!' And then she took a pinch of powder out of a little box and snapped her fingers above my head —"

"I saw that!"

"Well, you saw the rest, too. But what in the world did she mean, she'd 'just heard something'? . . ."

"I'll bet she heard something about Red that made her really understand what a crook he is," suggested Kerby. "Anyway, whatever it is, we won, and . . ."

Kerby's voice trailed off as he heard Bumps say, "Hey, would you look at those guys? What have *they* got to grin about, I'd like to know!"

They had nearly reached Red's house. Sitting in a row on the front steps were the Wildcats, and every one of them was grinning smugly.

Before anyone could say anything, an excited boy only a

little bit smaller than Willie came running out of the house. It was Bob Gibson.

"Willie! Hank!"

"What's the matter, Bob?"

"It's not a secret any more! They just told about it on the radio news!"

Willie and Hank grabbed each other and danced around.

"Wow!" said Willie. He looked greatly relieved as he glanced around and explained. "We couldn't talk about it to anyone, Dad said, till the news was officially released. But now it is."

"Talk about w-what?" stammered Bumps, sensing disaster.

Willie turned to him.

"I'm sorry, Bumps," he said, and he really did look sorry in a way, even though he was also very happy. "I guess we won't be around for the ball season after all. My dad's just been appointed to a big new job in Washington, so we're going to be moving down there."

His beefy shoulders slumping, his dreams of glory gone,

Bumps Burton trudged slowly homeward through the bitter cold.

"Just one game," he muttered. "If we could of had them three guys playing with us in just one game, even! . . ."

As for Kerby and Fenton, walking silently beside him, everything was clear now. They well knew now what it was Mrs. Graymalkin had 'just heard'— on the three o'clock radio newscast.

All the way home their general mood was funereal. But then, as the vacant lot come into sight, Fenton brightened up a bit.

"Well, we can't complain," he decided. "Things could be worse. We've still got our clubhouse, and that's something."

"Right!" agreed Kerby, eyeing it fondly. Then he grinned. "What's more, we've even got Louie Landowski!"

Bumps sighed. But after a moment he also managed to grin a little.

"Well, if we can just get him to play baseball as good as he plays hockey, we'll have something," he said. "And maybe we can! One thing is sure — the kid's all heart."